Jobeth

Teresa Lady

PublishAmerica
Baltimore

First printing

ISBN: 1-60836-195-0
PUBLISHED BY PUBLISHAMERICA, LLLP
www.publishamerica.com
Baltimore

Printed in the United States of America

This book is dedicated to Missy and Alix

Now there was a day when the sons (the angels) of God came to present themselves before the Lord, and Satan (the adversary and accuser) also came among them.

And the Lord said to Satan, From where did you come? Then Satan answered the Lord, From going to and fro on the earth and from walking up and down on it.

And the Lord said to Satan, Have you considered My servant Job, that there is none like him on the earth, a blameless and upright man, one who [reverently] fears God and abstains from and shuns evil [because it is wrong]?

Then Satan answered the Lord, Does Job [reverently] fear God for nothing?

Have You not put a hedge about him and his house and all that he has on every side? You have conferred prosperity and happiness upon him in the work of his hands, and his possessions have increased in the land.

But put forth Your hand now and touch all that he has, and he will curse You to Your face.

And the Lord said to Satan (the adversary and the accuser). Behold, all that he has is in your power, only upon the man himself put not forth your hand. So Satan went forth from the presence of the Lord.

Job 1:6-12 Amp.

The meeting was held in the usual place. The angels came to present themselves to their Lord. Satan also came.

"Where did you come from?" God asked him.

"Here and there," he retorted.

The Lord asked him if he had considered his daughter Jobeth.

"Why," he asked. "Do you think that she will continue to love you if I strike her down?"

"She is my beloved daughter," the Lord replied.

"For how long?" Satan asked.

"Test her if you dare," the Lord said. "Take what you can from her, but do not harm her."

Satan went away rejoicing. Gleefully he watched Jobeth on Sunday as she and her family entered the church and later after the service as they talked with other churchgoers as they came out of the building.

Look at her, he thought, so smug, so sure. She probably prays every day, too. Well not for long, he would see to that. He would wipe that smile right off of her face. When he was finished with her she would never pray again, or step a foot inside a church. And that faith that she clung to so steadfastly, well, not after he was finished with her.

Oh yes, it would be glorious, absolutely glorious. Happily, almost ecstatically he began to put his plan into action.

1

August 1983

As Jobeth Abbott prepared pancakes and sausages that Saturday morning, she never would have thought that it would be the last time that she would prepare that special breakfast for her four children. Pancakes and sausages on Saturday mornings had become something of a family tradition over the years in the Abbott household, begun while she and her husband, Bryce, were still newlyweds. While they were still dating, Bryce told her about his visits to his grandparents' house when he was growing up, where his grandmother would always prepare pancakes and sausage for his breakfast. Bryce considered that to be a grand treat given that his own mother's idea of breakfast was a bowl of cold cereal.

With that in mind, one Saturday morning shortly after they were married Jobeth decided to surprise him. The problem was that at the time her cooking skills were somewhat limited and she had never made pancakes before. Of course, she wanted them to be perfect for her new husband, but things did not go as planned. Bryce came into the kitchen that morning to find his new bride crying over a plate of burnt pancakes and sausages. He rushed to comfort her and in a grand gesture ate the entire plate, all the while exclaiming how good they were. Right then and there Jobeth decided that she was the luckiest girl in the world to have such a wonderful husband.

Twenty-one years later she still thought so. They had four wonderful children and a beautiful home. The kids were happy and healthy. Bryce was a senior partner at a large and successful law firm and she was the proprietor and manager of Jobeth's, a unique antique/gift/coffee shop.

With four children, her life was a busy one, but she enjoyed being a wife and a mother, and she felt confident in her abilities not only to maintain those roles, but at the same time to run her own business. Things did get hectic from time to time, but again, she was blessed to have a husband like Bryce. Despite his heavy caseload, and busy work schedule, he always made time for her and their children.

They had agreed before they married that they wanted four children. Jobeth has secretly wished for two boys and two girls, and her wish was granted when her two sons, Bradley, and then two years later, Keith came along, followed six years later by Kiera and two years after that, Nicole. As far as Jobeth was concerned they were the perfect family.

And, fortunately for them all, Jobeth's cooking skills had improved tremendously over the years.

After breakfast she assigned chores to Kiera and Nicole, after which she tackled the housework, while Bryce, Bradley and Keith started the yard work.

Later in the day they did some last minute shopping for school supplies. Bradley was leaving for college in a week and the other three would be returning to school the week after that. It was a typical Saturday in the Abbott household.

Later that evening, Bradley was going to take Keith and the two girls out for pizza. When they got ready to leave Bryce handed the keys to the car over to Bradley with the usual reminders to buckle up and drive carefully.

Keith was teasing his younger sisters as they walked out the door. Jobeth could hear the girls laughing at their brother. She watched out the kitchen window as they piled into the car, and she felt that familiar burst of pride she always felt when she looked at her children. Seeing them she was reminded once again what a truly blessed woman she was.

Bryce was laughing when he came back into the kitchen.

"I can't believe Brad will be gone in just a week," she said to him. "Where did the time go?"

"Well you know what they say," Bryce answered. "It flies when you're having fun. And it's been pretty great, hasn't it?"

"Absolutely," she said. "I'm just not sure I'm ready to start letting go."

"It's time, honey," Bryce said. "We can't keep them here with us forever."

"I know," she said. "But I'm going to miss him so much."

They talked about their upcoming trip to take Bradley to school the next week as she prepared pasta and garlic bread and Bryce cut up a salad for their dinner. Jobeth was still having trouble coming to terms with Bradley going to school so far from home, but at the same time she was excited about getting to spend some time alone with Bryce on the trip home. Keith, Kiera and Nicole were going to be staying with friends. It had been a couple of years since they had been away together, just the two of them. And as much as Jobeth loved her children, she also loved spending time with her husband.

After dinner they decided to go out for a movie.

"I'll leave the kids a note," she told Bryce. "They'll probably be home before we get back."

But when they returned home after the movie and a stop for ice cream, the kids still weren't home.

"I thought they'd be here by now," Bryce said.

"Me too," Jobeth said. "Maybe they decided to take in a movie too."

"Could be," Bryce said. "I'll check the answering machine to see if they called."

While he was checking the machine Jobeth heard a car pull up in the drive.

"That must be the kids," Jobeth said. But a moment later there was a knock at the door. Jobeth answered it to find Bill Riley, a deputy sheriff and a long time friend of Bryce's standing on their porch, and from the look on Bill's face she knew immediately he wasn't paying a social call.

Without inviting him in or even saying hello, she blurted out "What happened?" She could feel her stomach tightening with fear.

"Is Bryce here?" he asked her. She turned to get him but he was right behind her

"What's going on, Bill" Bryce asked. "Has something happened to the kids?"

"I'm afraid so," Bill said. He hesitated for a moment and then went on. "There's been an accident."

"How bad?" Jobeth asked. Her fear doubled as she waited for his reply.

"It's pretty bad," Bill said. "The kids have been taken to the hospital. I'll take you to them."

All the way to the hospital she and Bryce assured one another that the kids were fine and that everything was going to be all right. But the fact that Bill said nothing at all during the entire trip only made Jobeth more frightened.

It was a busy night in the hospital emergency room, but when Bill they told the woman at the desk who they were she called a nurse and they were immediately taken to a small private waiting room.

"The doctor will be right in," the nurse told them.

"But can't you tell us…" Jobeth started, but the nurse was already out the door.

A moment later a young doctor entered the room.

"Mr. and Mrs. Abbott?" he said.

"Yes. Our children?" they said in unison.

"I'm afraid I have some very bad news. Let's sit down" he said motioning toward the chairs. "Your children were involved in a serious automobile accident tonight. Their injuries were quite severe. We did everything we could, but we were unable to save them. I am terribly sorry."

"All four of them?" Jobeth whispered incredulously. "All four of them are dead?"

"I'm sorry," the doctor repeated. "We did everything we could."

After that Jobeth could hear Bryce and the doctor talking, but the rushing noise in her head and the onslaught of emotions that had begun to engulf her caused their voices to sound like they were coming from a great distance.

She knew that at some point Bill had taken them back home but she had only the vaguest memory of the trip. Bill came in with them, and he must have called his wife, Ann, because she came in shortly afterward. Jobeth remembered Ann embracing her and crying as she tried to speak soothing words, while Bill sat with Bryce. She had no idea how long they stayed. She was too numb to even cry. The tears would come later, but now she could do or say nothing. There were no words.

* * *

He had begun. How he enjoyed watching their suffering. He had done what he said he would do. He had wiped that smile right off of her face. And he was pleased with his work.

2

The next few days found them doing what Jobeth was certain had to be every parent's worst nightmare, planning their children's funeral. She had begun to experience feelings she had never known before, and certainly never wanted to experience again. Her grief was so overwhelming that it felt like a physical thing. It was like a great crushing weight, and at times she thought it might actually suffocate her.

When she learned that her children had died at the hands of a drunk driver who had walked away from the accident with a few minor cuts and scrapes, she also experienced a rage unlike anything she had ever imagined. She had never realized that she was capable of such anger. Her emotions teetered back and forth between the two emotions, grief and rage, while she went about the business of laying her beloved children to rest.

Friends and family came and went, bringing food and comforting words. While a part of her knew that they meant well, another part of her wanted to scream at them to just leave her alone. Nothing could comfort the pain that losing her children had caused. There were no words, no actions, no matter how well intended that could even begin to alleviate her suffering. The only thing that could do that was to see her babies again.

She, Keith, and the kids had attended church regularly for years and every week she thanked God for all that He had seen fit to bless her with. She always tried to remember how blessed she was, and to never forget the source of those blessings. Sometimes, when she would see someone going through a bad time, she would ask herself how easy would it be for her to hang on to her faith if she ever experienced bad times. She had sometimes asked herself how quick she would be to praise and thank God were she to loose even some what she had. Was her faith strong enough, she had asked herself more than once, to praise him in the bad times like she did in the good? Now that question was going to be answered and she wasn't sure what that answer would be.

She remembered a woman who had gone to her church when Bradley was a baby. Her name was Hannah Wilkinson. Hannah's only child, a ten year old girl, had died of leukemia. Hannah was beside herself with grief. Jobeth, being a new mother at the time had felt so badly for her. She and several other ladies from the church rallied round her, praying for her, helping her with her housework and errands, and just trying to be there for her in her time of trial as her friends and family were doing for her now. But Hannah was so overcome by her grief she just could not seem to get past it. After a while, she quit coming to church, and about a year later Jobeth heard that her marriage had broken up. Sometime later Hannah committed suicide. Jobeth remembered thinking at the time that if only Hannah's faith had been stronger. How naïve she had been, she thought now.

That had happened early in Jobeth's walk with the Lord. Neither she nor Bryce had been raised in church, but not long after they were married, a friend had invited them to a service at her church. They began attending regularly and soon after that they both committed themselves to the Lord. They had brought their four children up in the church. As the years went by Jobeth's faith grew stronger, as did Bryce's. And it was that faith that sustained them when Bryce's father died, and then Jobeth's died within months of one another.

Jobeth accredited the success of her business to her faith. Whenever she had a business decision, large or small to make, she always turned to God in prayer before proceeding. She prayed daily for her children and for Bryce, as well as her other family members, employees and friends.

The night before the funeral, as she lay in bed unable to sleep, she remembered the times that she had wondered if her faith was great enough to enable her to praise and give thanks to God in the bad times as she had in the good. She knew that she wanted it to be. *Please don't let me lose that too,* she prayed silently. *Not now, not when I need it the most.*

* * *

She hadn't quite given up yet. No matter. When she received no answer she would quit praying. He was certain of it. It was only a matter of time. He was a patient devil. He could wait.

3

Then his wife said to him, Do you still hold fast your blameless uprightedness? Renounce God and die. Job 2:9

Within a few weeks of the accident, Jobeth began to realize that instead of coming together in their time of crisis, she and Bryce had started to drift apart. In spite of their busy schedules and the demands of their work, they had always managed to make time for one another, usually in the morning before the kids got up. They would have a cup of coffee together and talk a few minutes before the early morning silence was shattered by the kids' arising. She had always enjoyed that quiet time together and she knew Bryce did as well. But since the funeral it seemed to her that Bryce had been avoiding her.

She couldn't remember a time since they had first met that they had been unable to think of something to talk about. Now when they were together they seemed to have nothing to say to one another. Bryce had also refused to go to church with her since the funeral.

One morning while he was preparing to leave for the office, he had seen Jobeth sitting in her sewing room with her Bible in her lap.

"What are you doing?" he had asked her.

"I'm praying," she said.

"Why?" he asked. "What is there to pray for now?"

"I'm praying for the strength to get through this," she said.

"Do you really think he's going to give it to you?" he said bitterly.

He turned and walked out of the room before she could reply. She started to go after him, but stopped when she realized that she didn't know what to say to him because she honestly didn't know the answer to his question. She only knew that she didn't know where else to turn but to God for the strength she needed.

* * *

He watched with pleasure as she and Bryce talked. Granted, she was still praying. She was a stubborn little thing, he would give her that. But not for long. He had already gotten to the husband. And that was half the battle. Soon, very soon.

4

Bryce's way of dealing with his grief was to throw himself into his work, so he returned to the office a few days after the funeral. He did not want to be at home where every room was a reminder of all that he had lost.

Jobeth's reaction to their loss was exactly the opposite. She could not bear to leave the house. She wanted to surround herself with her children's things. That, and her memories, was all she had left of them.

She could not bring herself to touch their bedrooms. Bradley's suitcase was still sitting in the corner of his room, opened, and partially packed, where he had begun preparing to leave for school. He had been looking forward to going to college. He had decided while he was still in elementary school that he wanted to be a doctor, and he had worked hard to get into a good college. They knew he had a long road ahead of him, but he was willing to work hard to achieve his goals. He had always been a good student and he wasn't afraid of hard work. He looked forward to the day when he would become a doctor, and it broke Jobeth's heart to know that now his dream would never be realized.

Keith's room was its usual mess, his bed unmade and his clothes and shoes scattered across the floor. Of the four, he was the messiest, and the one she always had to keep after the most to keep his room picked up. He was always assuring her that "he'd get to it" just as soon as he finished whatever he happened to be doing at the time. He would flash one of those big smiles of his at her, and no matter how aggravated she was her heart would melt. She would have given anything in the world for just one more of those smiles.

Kiera and Nicole shared a bedroom. They were each responsible for their half of the room and their side reflected their individual personalities. The summer before when Jobeth decided it was time for some fresh paint throughout the house, the girls argued over what colors they wanted. Bryce resolved the matter by painting half the room bright green, Kiera's choice, and the other half bright pink for Nicole.

During those long days after the funeral she found herself going from room to room. Sometimes she would have sworn she could still hear them. For just a brief moment it would be as it had been before, and then she would be brought back to the present and the ache in her heart would return. And once again she would pray, *Please Lord, please give me the strength to get through this.*

Other times she would find herself thinking about the driver of the car that had caused the accident. She knew he was a young man, not much older than Bradley had been, and that his name was Jake Ellis. She also knew that he had escaped the accident with only minor injuries. In fact, he hadn't even had to spend a night in the hospital. That fact enraged Jobeth. To think that he had ended the lives of her four beautiful children while walking away without only a few cuts and scrapes was intolerable. She wanted him to suffer like she was suffering. She had never been a vengeful person, but now she wanted revenge. She wanted Jake Ellis to pay for what he had done. She wanted him to feel the pain that she was feeling. She wanted him to know what it felt like to loose the most important thing in his life.

At times she found herself growing angry with God for allowing this to happen to her. Why, she would cry, why would you allow my beautiful children to die, while the one who caused their deaths escaped with not only his life, but with no physical injuries at all? How can this be? Then, in the next breath, she would be begging Him to forgive her anger.

* * *

He could feel her anger, and it was wonderful. And then she turned to prayer again, begging for forgiveness. You foolish woman, he thought. Why do you continue to turn to him? He can't help you now. He would not allow her to defeat him.

5

She thought often of Hannah Wilkinson. Now she truly understood her grief, and how easy it would be to just let go like Hannah had done.

But despite her pain, there was still a tiny part of her that wanted to get through this thing, to not only survive it, but to live again. She knew this was what her children would want for her. She remembered when her father died, how sad she had been. Her children had gathered round her then. Nicole, the youngest, had climbed onto her lap and said, "Please don't cry, mommy. I can't stand for you to be so sad." Then the others had gathered round, comforting her. She could almost hear Nicole's sweet voice now, telling her not to cry, not to be sad. It was so hard not to be, but she knew they would not want this for her or their father.

Her mind went back time and time again to that last day, reliving every detail of it, their Saturday morning pancake breakfast, doing housework with her daughters while the boys worked outdoors with Bryce. She remembered how excited they were about going out for pizza with their brothers that night. At eight and ten years old, the two girls adored their older brothers, and the brothers loved their little sisters. Bradley took his position as the oldest very seriously. He always looked out for the two girls as well as Keith. Keith was the clown, always teasing and playing tricks on them and they loved it.

She remembered watching them pile into the car when they were leaving that evening, and the burst of pride she had felt watching them.

She found herself thinking about stories about tragic events that she had read over the years. One story in particular kept coming to mind about a mother of teenage twin daughters who were going to a concert with some friends. The day of the concert the mother awoke with a feeling of dread that she could not shake, and as the day wore on, it only grew worse. Finally, convinced it was a warning, she refused to let the girls go with their friends to the concert. Of course the daughters were furious with her, they had been looking forward to going for weeks. But the mother was convinced she had done the right thing, and as it turned out, she was right. The daughters' friends were killed on the way home from the concert in an automobile accident.

Why, Jobeth asked, herself, had she had no such premonition? She had been a good mother, always trying to stay in tune with her children's needs. Why?

But there had been no warning, no premonition, and she had let her babies go out that night, never even considering that it would be the last time she would ever see them.

6

In her absence from the store, her employees had kept it running and kept her informed of what was going on, and she was grateful for their help. The people she had chosen to work for her were more than just her employees, they were her friends as well, and they all loved the shop as much as she did so she knew the store was in good hands.

She had always loved antiques, and with Bryce's encouragement, she had started a small antique shop soon after they were married. A few years later when the building next to her shop became available she expanded her business and added a gift shop and a coffee shop.

Jobeth hired only people who knew antiques and shared her love for them to work with the antique customers, while the gift shop was manned by two women Jobeth had known most of her life, Carol Jordan and Kate Hansen. Both of them enjoyed working with the public and shared Jobeth's flair for making just the right selection for each customer. The coffee shop was run by Jenny Scott, another longtime friend.

A few weeks after the funeral, Kate, who Jobeth had put in charge during her absence, began to gently question her about when she was planning to come back to work. At first Jobeth put her off, but in her usual kind, but persistent way, Kate kept at it until Jobeth agreed to start coming in for at least a couple of hours each day. She knew her friend was right and she needed to start getting out. Once she did, she realized how much she had missed working and it was not long until she was back to working full time. The pain over losing her children had by no means diminished, but she was learning to bear it.

It was on a Friday night several weeks after Jobeth had returned to work and like a lot of the other downtown businesses they stayed open later than usual that night. Jobeth had left Kate and Jenny at the shop while she ran a few errands. She was on her way back when she heard what sounded like an explosion, and within minutes, sirens. As she neared the shop she could see the street had already been blocked off by fire trucks. But she could see from where she was that her shop was on fire. She jumped out of her car and hurried toward the shop, but was stopped by a police officer.

"That's my store," she told him. "Two of my employees are in there."

"You have to stay back and let the firefighters do their work," he said.

So she watched as the store she had built from nothing burnt to the ground before her eyes. But what was far worse than losing the store was learning that neither Kate nor Jenny had made it out of the store. The same police officer who had stopped her earlier was walking her back to her car when Bryce came running through the crowd that had gathered.

"Are you all right?" he asked her. "I heard about the fire on the news."

"I'm fine," she sobbed. "But Kate and Jenny were in the store."

"I'm so sorry," he said. "Let me take you home."

"I have my car," she said.

"We'll get it later," he said.

"It's okay," she said. "I can drive."

He didn't argue with her.

That night she lay in bed sleepless and numb with despair. She was losing everything that she held dear, and she didn't know how to stop it. She couldn't help but wonder if her marriage would be the next thing to go.

* * *

Oh, he'd done it this time. He was so excited he wanted to dance with joy. She had tried to hang on, but now, now she had seen there was nothing to hang onto. Now she would understand.

7

She was sitting at the table the next morning staring at a cup of cold coffee when Bryce came in.

"I'm so sorry about your friends, and the store," he said to her. "Do you want me to stay home with you? I was just going to go in for a couple of hours, but I don't have to."

"No, that's okay," she said. "There's nothing you can do here. Do you want some coffee?"

"No, that's all right," he said. "I'll have some at the office."

She didn't know if it was her imagination working overtime or not, but she was certain she heard relief in his voice when she told him he didn't have to stay with her. But at that point she was too distraught to care. She just wanted to be alone.

He started toward the door, but then turned back and said," You're sure you don't want me to stay here with you."

"I'm sure," she said. "Go on to work."

"I'll be back in a couple of hours," he said.

He was out the door and in his car before it occurred to her that he hadn't kissed her goodbye. When she thought about it, she couldn't remember when he had last kissed her at all. Before the accident he never left the house without a goodbye kiss. But that was before. Everything had changed now.

Three days later she found herself once again at the funeral home, now burying two close friends. She also found herself praying once more not to let this cause her to lose her faith.

When she saw Kate and Jenny's families she wanted so badly to find some comforting words to say to them. But the worlds would not come. The funerals were being held at different funeral homes. Viewing had been scheduled for the same time, with the two funerals the next day, Kate's in the morning and Jenny's in the afternoon. Jobeth went to Kate's viewing first, but when she saw Kate's husband, and daughter with her husband and two small children she froze. As much as she wanted to, she could not bring herself to speak to them. She knew what they were going through, she grieved for Kate too. They had been friends for years, and Kate had been there for her when her children died. And yet now she was unable to comfort her friend's family.

The same was true at Jenny's viewing. Again, she found herself standing at the back of the funeral home, unable to even speak to Jenny's family.

* * *

He was winning, he could feel it. She was giving up. That precious faith of hers that she had so stubbornly clung to was almost gone. She couldn't talk to those people because she knew it was all her fault. She couldn't tell them that everything would be all right and that God would help them through. She couldn't tell them that because she didn't believe it herself.

He laughed with glee.

8

Right away people began asking her if she planned to rebuild the shop, but she did not have the strength or the desire to even make a decision like that. So her answer, when anyone asked was simply that she was still considering her options. But as far as she was concerned there were no more options.

She had tried to pull herself together after the accident. She had prayed for strength. She had gone back to work and she had been working hard to get her life back in order. But losing the shop and her two dear friends, particularly so quickly after the children's deaths was almost more than she could bear. She found it harder and harder to hang on to her faith. For a short while she had begun to believe that she would able to survive that tragedy. But she did not think she had it within herself to survive anymore heartache. There was only so much that a person could bear, she thought, and I've reached my limit.

In a few short months she had gone from being a happily married mother of four and a successful business owner to an angry, grief-stricken shell of a woman. In fact, when she looked in the mirror, she hardly recognized herself anymore. Slim to begin with, she had lost more weight than she could afford to lose, and she had started to see some gray hairs. Well, I feel years older, she told herself, why shouldn't I look it?

9

Her marriage continued to deteriorate during that period. It was no more Bryce's fault than it was her own, she realized. They each had their own way of dealing with their grief and because of that they were unable to help one another through that dark time. The loss of their children had left too big of a hole in their lives, and at that point both of them were so engrossed in their own grieving process that they didn't have anything left to give to their marriage.

About a month after the explosion, Bryce came home one night with some unexpected news.

"I've been asked to go to London for a few weeks to set up a new office over there," he told her.

"I didn't know the firm had planned to expand abroad," she said.

"They've been talking about it for some time now," he said. "We have offices in several large cities here in the states. The partners felt it was time to expand even further."

"How long would you be gone?" she asked him.

"A few weeks, I'm not quite sure yet," he said. "You could come with me."

"I don't think so," she replied. "I don't think I'm up for a trip like that right now."

Once again, she would have sworn she saw relief in his eyes.

"Well, maybe you could come over for a week or so anyway?" he suggested. "It's up to you."

"I'll think about it," she told him. But she knew she wouldn't go. She didn't want to and she knew he didn't really want her to. "When will you be leaving?"

"At the end of the week," he said.

He was leaving. She knew it was a business trip, but she couldn't help but feel that it was more than that. He was obviously anxious for the chance to get away. And she had to admit she was glad he was going. She didn't know what to say to him anymore, and she didn't have the strength or energy to try. As much as she hated to think that their marriage might be coming to an end, she could not bring herself to fight to save it. She had nothing left to fight with. She still loved Bryce, but at that point her grief and despair were much stronger than her love or her desire to save their marriage.

* * *

The husband was leaving—perfect. Things could not have worked out any better. She was alone. He would make sure he stayed that way.

10

The rest of the week she helped him get ready for the trip. It wasn't the first business trip he had taken in their marriage, but it was the first time that she was anxious to see him go. The day that he left she offered to drive him to the airport, but he insisted on taking a cab. As she watched the cab pull away from the curb, she realized that he hadn't told her when he would be back, or given her a number where he could be reached.

"I'll call when I get settled," was all he had said as he gave her a quick kiss before hurrying out to the cab.

When he did call, although she was home, she let the machine pick up. His message was brief, the name of the hotel where he was staying and two numbers where he could be reached.

"Call me if you need anything," he said.

But what she needed he couldn't give her, because the only thing she needed was to have her children back and her life to go back to being the way that it was before.

Again, the meeting was held in the usual place. And again God asked him, "Where did you come from?"

"Here and there," he replied.

"Have you thought about my daughter Jobeth? She still loves me, you know."

"Of course she does now, but were she to be afflicted, how long would that love last then?"

"We shall see," God said. "Only don't let her die."

He was almost beside himself with joy as he left. This was it. He had worn her down, he had taken everything from her, and still she clung to her faith. But now, now she would learn what real suffering was. And there would be no more praying, no more faith, no more love. He had her this time.

11

Again there was a day when the sons of God [the angels] came to present themselves before the Lord, and Satan (the adversary and the accuser) came also among them to present himself before the Lord.

And the Lord said to Satan, From where do you come? And Satan (the adversary and the accuser) answered the Lord, From going to and fro on the earth and from walking up and down on it.

And the Lord said to Satan, Have you considered My servant Job, that there is none like him on the earth, a blameless and upright man, one who [reverently] fears God and abstains from and shuns all evil [because it is wrong]? And still he holds fast his integrity, although you moved Me against him to destroy him without cause?

Then Satan answered the Lord, Skin for skin! Yes, all that a man has will he give for his life.

But put forth Your hand now, and touch his bone and flesh, and he will curse and renounce You to Your face.

And the Lord said to Satan, Behold he is in your hand; only spare his life.

Job 2:1-6 Amp.

Jobeth was in the shower a few days later when she first noticed the lump in her right breast. Her first reaction was to ignore it. She had already lost everything that had any meaning to her anyway, her children, her friends, her store. But in spite of all that she had been through in the past months, when faced with the possibility that she could be facing a serious if not fatal illness she could not bring herself to give up. So she made an appointment with her doctor to have it checked. Somehow she was not surprised when the results of the biopsy came back positive.

A few days later as she was leaving the doctor's office after hearing the test results she ran into one of her closest friends, Ellie Steele. When Ellie asked her to come and have coffee with her, Jobeth agreed. During the course of the conversation she blurted out the reason she had been to the doctor.

"Jobeth, I'm so sorry," Ellie told her. "What can I do for you?"

"Nothing," Jobeth said. "There's nothing you can do."

"Well, Bryce will come home," Ellie said. "You have told him about this haven't you?"

"Not yet," Jobeth said.

"Well you need to go home right now and call him," Ellie said. "Listen, I'll tell you what. I'll call Billie and Zoey and we'll come over tonight and keep you company."

"You don't have to do that," Jobeth said.

"Yes, we do," Ellie said. "You can't go through this by yourself, and even if you call Bryce as soon as you get home, it will be quite a while before he can get home. I'll call the girls as soon as I got home. We'll stop and pick up a pizza or something, so don't worry about dinner."

Without giving her a chance to protest, or make any excuses for them not to come, Ellie hurried off, leaving Jobeth wondering why she had told Ellie about her doctor's visit in the first place.

12

That night when her friends arrived it was obvious right away that Ellie had already told the others about Jobeth's trip to the doctor. Though they didn't come right out and say anything, she could tell by the way they greeted her they knew, each giving her a very gentle hug as if they were afraid of squeezing her too hard. That and the look on their faces said it all. At first she wished Ellie hadn't said anything. But then she realized that by doing so, Ellie had saved her the trouble of having to say those horrible words "I have a lump in my breast" and for that she was grateful.

"Did you call Bryce?" Ellie asked.

"I left him a message to call," she lied. She hadn't been able to bring herself to call him just yet.

The three of them made themselves at home, setting the table and getting the food they had brought ready.

"You really didn't have to go to all that trouble," she told them.

"It's no trouble," Zoey said. "We're your friends. We want to be here for you."

"Of course we do," said Billie. "What are friends for? And with Bryce away, you really shouldn't be here by yourself."

"No, you shouldn't," said Ellie, giving her a hug.

The three of them tried to keep up a stream of light conversation as they sat down to eat. But half way through the meal Ellie turned to the subject they had been skirting around since they arrived.

"So when will you be going in for the surgery?" she asked in her usual blunt way.

"What?" Jobeth said.

"The mastectomy," Ellie replied. "That's what you're going to do, isn't it?"

"I suppose," Jobeth said. "I'll go back to see the doctor day after tomorrow."

"Well I don't know how you've done it," Billie said.

"Done what?" Jobeth asked her.

"Held up under all this, first the kids, then the store, then Bryce leaving, and now this," Billie said.

"I'd have to say that the Lord has seen fit to give me the strength I need," she said. "But let me clarify something. Bryce is away on business."

"Of course he is, dear," Zoey said. "I'm sure Billie didn't mean anything by that."

"Of course I didn't," Billie responded. "But after all that's happened, he certainly couldn't have picked a worse time to go abroad."

"He didn't pick this time," Jobeth said. "This expansion has been in the works for some time now."

"Enough about that," Ellie said. "We're here to comfort our friend, not talk about where Bryce should or shouldn't be right now. Jobeth has more important things to worry about right now than everyone's speculations about where her marriage is headed."

"What is that supposed to mean?" Jobeth asked.

"Nothing, nothing at all," Ellie said. "I'm just saying you've got more important things to contend with right now than idle gossip."

"People are gossiping about my marriage?" she said incredulously.

"Well statistics do show that a lot of marriages can't withstand the loss of a child," said the ever tactful Zoey.

"I'm going to say this one time, and one time only. Bryce and I have not separated. He is in London on business. End of discussion," said Jobeth.

"Yes, dear."

"Of course."

"Whatever you say, sweetie."

Once again the conversation turned to the mundane, but only briefly before Ellie turned it back to the fire at the shop.

"Did they ever find out what caused the fire?" Ellie asked.

"Apparently there was a gas leak," Jobeth said.

"Such a shame," said Billie. "Two lives lost, not to mention all the work you put into the place. Do you plan to rebuild?"

"I don't know," Jobeth said. "I was starting to look into it when this other thing came up. I guess I'll have to see how this works out before I make any other plans."

Billie shook her head. "So much trouble. It's almost like you're…I don't know…like you're being punished."

"What?" said Jobeth. "Are you saying you think I've done something to deserve all of this?"

"Well, one can't help but wonder," Zoey said. "All these things happening, one right after another."

"I'll admit I'm not perfect," Jobeth said. "I'm a sinner, just like everyone else. And these past few months have been the worst in my life. I've experienced a loss I don't think I'll ever recover from. There isn't a day that goes by that I don't think about my children. I'll never stop thinking about them or Kate and Jenny, or missing all of them. But God is not punishing me. I don't believe that. I refuse to believe that."

"Well then, if you don't mind my asking," said Billie. "Why do you think all of this has happened?"

"Let's just change the subject, girls," said Ellie. "We're upsetting Jobeth. That's not what we came here to do."

"No, it's all right," Jobeth said. "I've asked myself that question a million times, and I'm no closer to finding an answer than I was to begin with. I don't know why any of this happened. I never will. I don't think I'm supposed to know. My job, I think, is just to trust in God to get me through it."

"Can you do that?" Zoey asked. "I think if I lost my children I would just want to die too."

"I always thought that too," Jobeth said. "Once they were born, I couldn't imagine my life without them. And to be honest, when I first found the lump in my breast, I seriously considered just letting nature take its course instead of seeing the doctor. But I realized I couldn't do that. And when he told me it was cancerous, I was scared. In spite of everything I don't want to die. I know I have to fight this thing. It's what the kids and Kate and Jenny would want me to do. It's not up to me to decide when it's time for me to die, it's up to God. Just like it was for the kids and Kate and Jenny."

* * *

This was wonderful, absolutely glorious. Now her friends were questioning her, gossiping about her. Her husband was gone, her friends were turning on her, she was all alone, and soon she would no longer be able to resist him at all.

13

Long after her friends left that evening Jobeth sat in her silent house thinking back over their conversation. Though she hadn't wanted the company, and at first she had taken offense in some of what they had to say, she had to admit to herself that she was glad they had come. It was the first time she had actually talked about what had been happening to her those past few months. Up until then he had been forcing herself through each day, trying to put up a brave front, praying for the strength to just get through the days. Now she realized she needed more than to just get through this time of trial. She needed the assurance that she could face this period of testing and come out on the other side, a stronger better person for having done so. And she knew exactly where to turn. In her darkened living room, she turned to God in prayer and as she did she could feel at long last his comforting presence.

Later, feeling more alive than she had felt in months, she called her husband. It was time they talked.

"I'm so glad to hear your voice," was the first thing he said to her.

"We need to talk," she said. Briefly she told him what had been going on since he left.

"I'll catch the next flight out of here," he said.

"I'll be waiting for you," she told him. "Bryce?"

"Yes."

"I love you."

"I love you too."

It was the first time either of them had spoken those words since before the children died. She didn't realize how much she missed hearing those words until she heard him say them.

* * *

No, no, no, no! This can't be happening. After all that he'd done to her, she was still praying.

"Noooooooooooooooo," he screamed.

14

Bryce was with her when she went in for the surgery. The night before she went to the hospital they knelt together in prayer. It was the first time they had done so since their children died. When they were finished she could see that there were tears in Bryce's eyes. Gently, she reached out to him. "Bryce?"

"That's the first time I've prayed since the accident," he said' "I've just been so angry. That morning I saw you praying I couldn't believe it. I couldn't imagine how you could turn to God after what had happened."

"Those are the times when we need him the most," she said.

"I know that now," he said. "I don't want to be angry anymore."

"I don't either," she said as he took her into his arms. For the first time since the night their children died they comforted one another.

The next morning he drove her to the hospital.

"Are you scared?" he asked her on the way.

"A little," she said.

"Me too," he said, squeezing her hand.

He was waiting in the waiting room when the doctor, looking a little sheepish came out to inform him that, as he put it,"there must have been some kind of mistake. You wife doesn't have cancer. She's fine."

Bryce smiled. Somehow the doctor's news didn't surprise him at all, and he was sure it wouldn't Jobeth either. He knew there had been no mistake. Just an answer to a prayer.

He took her home the next morning.

"After the accident," Bryce told her when they got home from the hospital. "I couldn't stand to be here. Everything reminded me of them, including you. It was just too hard."

Once the lines of communication were open, they were able to talk and comfort one another, and most importantly, to pray together. They both knew that there would be rough times ahead, but now they were going to go through them together.

With Bryce's help, she began to rebuild Jobeth's. The grand re-opening was bittersweet for Jobeth. While she looked forward to working in her shop again, memories of her two lost were friends were ever close. But she felt certain that this is what Kate and Jenny would have wanted her to do. In fact, she could almost feel their presence the day of the re-opening, and she was comforted by it.

That night, after she closed the store, she called both Kate and Jenny's families, and made arrangements to see them. She felt she owed them both an apology, and she wanted to see how they were doing. At each home she was welcomed, and for that she was grateful. She had been racked with guilt over her behavior at Kate and Jenny's funerals but both families assured her that there was no reason for her to feel that way. They understood what she had gone through. Before she left each home they prayed together. Jobeth asked the Lord to give them the strength that he had given to her to get through their time of trial, and she knew that prayer would be answered.

Though her life could never go back to the way it was before, she had survived some tremendous blows and come back from them a stronger person, her faith intact.

Even her marriage had grown stronger since Bryce's return from London. Now that they had both realized how very much they needed one another they had become closer than they had ever been. In many ways it was like falling in love all over again, only this time it was not the passionate all-consuming splendor of first love, but a deeper, abiding love born out of trial and heartache. It was a lasting love, almost spiritual in nature. And it seemed to grow deeper every day.

Bryce also began going to church with her again.

"I'm so glad you came with me today," she told him after the first Sunday he went with her.

"So am I," he said. "I didn't realize how much I missed it."

* * *

He could not understand it. Not only had she kept her faith, but her husband's had been restored as well. It made no sense at all to him.

15

About three months after the re-opening, Jobeth came down with what she first thought was the flu. But when her symptoms didn't disappear after a few days, Bryce insisted that she see the doctor. Neither of them was prepared for the doctor's diagnosis. She was two months pregnant. The thought had never even occurred to her. And she could tell by the look on Bryce's face, he hadn't thought of it either. But by the time they got home, surprise was beginning to give way to excitement and joy for both of them.

The next morning Jobeth arose early. As she began making the coffee, it occurred to her that it was Saturday. In light of the joyful news they had received the day before, she decided it was time to renew an old family tradition. When Bryce came down the first thing he said was, "Is that sausage I smell?"

She flipped a pancake on the griddle and turned to him with a smile. "It will be a while before this one can share this with us," she said, pointing to her stomach. "But I think it's time for us to renew this family tradition."

As her child grew inside of her, Jobeth remembered her other pregnancies and the births of her other children. Though the memories were now tinged with sadness, it was comforting to know that she was beginning to be able to think of her children with happiness now. At first, each time she thought of one of them, she was so saddened that even the happiest and funniest memories would bring her to tears. But now, though she still missed them terribly, and knew that she always would, she was beginning to enjoy those precious memories.

Something else that happened during that time was that the vengeful thoughts she had had about the young man who caused the accident were beginning to fade. She knew he was in prison. Now she began to wonder about him, was he remorseful for what he had done? What kind of a person was he? And slowly, gently, but with increasing persistence, that still, small voice inside of her began to speak. *It's time,* it said; *time to face him, time to forgive.* At first, she tried to resist, but the voice grew stronger, until she could ignore it no longer. She told Bryce what she was feeling.

"We have to go see him," she told Bryce.

"I don't know if I can face him," Bryce said. "And I'm not sure it's a good idea for you to see him, especially now of all times."

"I have to do this," she said. "Will you come with me?"

"Of course I will," he told her.

So they went to the prison to see the young man who had stolen their children's lives.

When the young man saw them, he immediately burst into tears.

"I've wanted to see you ever since…" he said. "To try to explain. To tell you how sorry I am."

The night of the accident, he told them, his fiancée had broken their engagement. Upset, he had stopped at a bar. He didn't ordinarily drink very much, but he was so upset that he just kept drinking.

"I should have called a cab," he told them. "Or better yet, not gone into the bar in the first place. But I didn't and I did. There isn't a day that goes by that I don't think about what I've done. And I'm sure there never will be."

Before the visit was over, Jobeth and Bryce both forgave him, and as the broken young man sobbed uncontrollably, they both prayed for him. As they did Jobeth felt a sense of peace about her like nothing she had never known before, and from the look on Bryce's face she could tell that he felt it too.

16

Seven months later they welcomed Emily Elizabeth Abbott home. Jobeth found it almost impossible to keep her eyes off of her new baby daughter. Her heart was bursting with love for this beautiful child that the Lord had seen fit to give her. Of course Emily couldn't take the place of the others, nor could she replace the joy the other children had brought into Jobeth's and Bryce's lives. But they knew that wasn't why she had been given to them.

That night after they laid her in her bed for the first time, they took each other's hand and prayed over her as she drifted off to sleep. They prayed for guidance in raising her, they gave thanks for her, and for the joy they knew that she would bring to their lives.

Jobeth remembered the times that she had wondered how quick she would be to praise God and give thanks if she were ever faced with hard times, and now she knew the answer to that question. She knew that she would never stop praising Him or giving thanks, in good times or in bad. Because she knew now that he would be with her, no matter where she was. Looking into the face of her beautiful new baby daughter, she could see His love for her, strong and steadfast as it had always been. And once again she gave thanks.

* * *

He had been defeated. He didn't know how, but she had defeated him.

He went back to the meeting place.

"Why?" he screamed.

"Her heart is pure."

"I made her suffer."

"I helped her bear that suffering."

"I took everything that she had."

"Not everything, oh no, not everything."

17

2008

Jobeth and Bryce hurried into the hospital. Even after all those years, seeing this place made her heart lurch and brought back the painful memories of the night more than 25 years earlier when they had hurried to this very place only to learn that their four children had died.

But this time they were here for a joyous occasion. Their son-in-law, Ryan, had called them early that morning at their cabin where they had gone to spend a long weekend. Emily was in labor and he had taken her to the hospital. But the baby wasn't due for three more weeks.

"I knew we should have stayed in town," she told Bryce as they hurried into the building.

"The baby wasn't due for three more weeks," Bryce said. "And Emily assured us she was fine."

"I know, I know," she said. "I just hope everything's all right."

Ryan met them when they got off the elevator.

"Come," he said. "Wait till you see." He was clearly bursting with excitement.

They followed him down the hallway and into Emily's hospital room. She looked up at them, her smile so radiant it seemed to light up the entire room. Then Jobeth looked at what Emily was holding in her arms.

"Oh my God," she said. "It's..."

"Twins," Emily said. "And the doctor never detected it. Come, meet your new grandchildren."

Jobeth, with Bryce right behind her, rushed to their daughter, who held two bundles in her arm, one pink and one blue.

"They're beautiful," Jobeth cried.

Laying the pink bundle on her lap, Emily took the blue one and held him out to her father.

"This is your grandson, Bradley Keith," she said. Then taking the pink bundle she handled it to her mother, "And this is your granddaughter, Keira Nicole."

Jobeth felt tears of joy as she took her new granddaughter into her arms.

"Welcome, little girl," she said, kissing the baby's forehead. "Nana is so happy to finally meet you." She looked at Bryce, who was talking softly to his new grandson.

Ryan was standing by Emily's bedside, his arms around his wife, the joy on both of their faces so clear and so radiant Jobeth almost felt she could reach out and touch it.

There had been a time in her life when Jobeth would never have believed that she would ever know joy and happiness again, a time when her life seemed broken beyond repair. She had known loss and she had known heartache. But through it all, there had been someone there, at her side, sustaining her, giving her the strength to bear what she needed to bear. Now, all these many years later, He was still with her in her times of trial and her times of happiness. As she looked into the eyes of her new granddaughter, her greatest wish for her and her brother was that they know Him too.

Printed in the United States
138063LV00001B/132/P

9 781608 361953